THE
GIANT
BEAR

AN INUIT FOLKTALE

Published by Inhabit Media Inc.

www.inhabitmedia.com

Nunavut Office   P.O. Box 11125, Iqaluit, Nunavut, X0A 1H0
Ontario Office   146A Orchard View Blvd., Toronto, Ontario, M4R 1C3

Edited by: Louise Flaherty and Neil Christopher
Written by: Jose Angutinngurniq
Art Direction by: Neil Christopher
Illustrations by: Eva Widermann

We acknowledge the support of the Canada Council for the Arts for our publishing program.

Printed and bound in Hong Kong
by Paramount Printing Co. • June 2012 #133396

Library and Archives Canada Cataloguing in Publication

Angutinngurniq, Jose

The giant bear : an Inuit folktale / by Jose Angutinngurniq ; illustrated by Eva Widermann.

ISBN 978-1-927095-03-4

1. Inuit--Folklore. 2. Oral tradition--Nunavut.
I. Widermann, Eva II. Title.

E99.E7A534 2012   j398.24'529780899712   C2012-900637-8

**Canada Council   Conseil des Arts
for the Arts   du Canada**

THE GIANT BEAR

AN INUIT FOLKTALE

Told by
Jose Angutinngurniq

Illustrated by
Eva Widermann

FOREWORD

Inuit ancestors lived in a very different world. When we listen to the stories that have been passed from generation to generation, we catch glimpses of this ancient time. We are told that when the world was much younger, many strange beings populated the circumpolar regions of the world. Great giants moved across the Arctic landscape; malevolent ogresses hunted the small and the weak; shy marine races hid below the protective sea ice waiting for an opportunity to steal children; and countless other preternatural things crawled, swam, flew, and lived in this ancient place. We are told that some live here still.

One of these powerful creatures is mentioned in the traditional stories of many of the Arctic regions—the giant polar bear. Some storytellers refer to these giant marine beasts as ice-covered bears on account of their heavily iced fur. In other regions, however, these giant marine animals are known as the nanurluit (nanurluk singular).

So massive were these animals, that they are often compared to the huge icebergs that populate the Arctic waters. These colossal bears were powerful swimmers and could also move quickly over land. The nanurluit were the only prey that offered the great Arctic giants any sport. You see, the great giants could walk across rivers and kick over mountains. Regular polar bears seemed like helpless lemmings to them and whales were as fragile as sculpin in their hands. The giants craved the excitement that came from hunting creatures as powerful as themselves.

For a while this legendary world was held in balance—giant bears with equally powerful giants to hunt them, keeping their numbers in check. But eventually the world changed. The great giants began to disappear. There were few of these mighty hunters left to hunt the nanurluit. And for a short time, these ursine behemoths had no predators and were able to hunt in Arctic seas and coastal areas without challenge.

The nanurluit had huge appetites to go with their massive bodies. They hunted whales, seals, walrus, and everything else they could get into their mouths, including Inuit. Due to the nanurluit's size, these bears were almost invulnerable to the attacks of Inuit. Some stories even tell us that their fur was so heavily covered by ice that even arrows and harpoons could not penetrate it. This icy armour, coupled with the bear's size, strength, and speed, made the nanurluit greatly feared.

As feared and invulnerable as these giant bears may have been, they could still be killed. Several stories tell us how Inuit outsmarted this colossal foe, as you will see in the following story shared by well-known storyteller Jose Angutinngurniq.

Neil Christopher
Iqaluit, Nunavut

PRONUNCIATION GUIDE

Aglu (ag-loo)
A breathing hole in sea ice that is created or kept open by a marine animal.

Iglu (Ig-loo)
A winter dwelling made with snow blocks.

Nanurluk (na-nur-look)
A giant polar bear.

Nanurluit (na-nur-lew-eet)
Giant polar bears (plural).

My grandfather was full of stories. Some of the stories I cannot remember, but there are some that I can.

And this is one of them.

There was once a husband and wife living alone by the sea.

However, as they soon found out, the couple was not really alone.

One day, while out hunting for seals, the man found a large hole in the sea ice.

When he looked down into the hole, he could see a giant bear sleeping deep in the water.

This bear was a nanurluk, and this hole in the ice was the nanurluk's aglu, an opening that it kept clear of ice so that it could breathe. But breathing was not the only use the bear had for this aglu. It would also use this hole to climb out of the water and onto the ice to hunt.

The man knew that, no matter how capable a hunter he was, facing a nanurluk head-on would be very dangerous. He would have to devise a plan to protect his camp.

The man did not want to be spotted by the nanurluk, so he crouched low next to the opening of the aglu and began scooping water out of the hole and letting it pour over the icy sides of the aglu. Slowly the water froze, and the walls of the nanurluk's aglu became thicker and thicker, making the hole in the ice smaller and smaller.

The man then pushed snow into the open water of the hole, slowly filling it, until the hole was very narrow, too narrow for the nanurluk to fit through.

Then, he retreated to his camp and told his wife of the monster living under the ice and of his plan. The two of them worked quickly, pouring water onto their iglu's entrance and walls. In the cold air, the water hardened the snow, making the iglu thicker and stronger. The couple hoped that this would protect them if the bear came to their camp.

When they were satisfied with their work, the hunter gathered his knife and harpoon and started to make his way back towards the aglu to face the sleeping bear. As he left, he asked his wife to stay inside this ice-covered iglu, where it would be safer.

Now the ice around the nanurluk's aglu was thick and strong—and the walls of the man's iglu were just as thick and just as strong.

The hunter knew what he had to do next.

As he neared the aglu, readying his knife
and his harpoon, the hunter whispered to
himself, "Now I will let the nanurluk know
what I have done."

The man took a deep breath, then leaned forward so that his shadow fell onto the giant bear's face. He wanted the bear to notice him, and eventually the nanurluk became aware of his presence.

As soon as the nanurluk spotted the hunter, it quickly
swam up to its aglu. But, just as the hunter had hoped,
the hole was too narrow for the bear to pass through.
It viciously clawed at the newly frozen ice, and slowly,
the hole began to widen.

After a few moments of clawing at the ice, the nanurluk tried to climb through the hole, but it was only wide enough for the huge bear's head.

This was just what the hunter had hoped for.

As soon as he saw the monster's head, he used his harpoon to stab at its eyes and nose.

Soon the nanurluk was bleeding badly.

Enraged, the nanurluk continued to claw furiously at the hole.

Every time the hunter had the chance, he slashed and stabbed at the huge bear. He knew that the nanurluk would soon free itself from the ice. This would be his only chance to wound the giant.

Finally, the nanurluk pulled itself out onto the ice.

Face to face with the huge bear, the hunter thought about running, but he did not.

The bear was bleeding badly and didn't seem to see or smell the hunter. Confused, it growled, then simply turned and wandered away.

The hunter was then certain that the bear could not see him or track his scent, so he followed the huge footprints and the trail of blood across the ice and onto the land.

The hunter tracked the nanurluk as it stumbled across the landscape. Blind and without the ability to smell, the great bear ambled slowly, without direction, across the land.

Eventually, the nanurluk collapsed onto the ground.

Several hours later, the hunter found the huge bear's body. The meat from this bear would provide him and his wife with food for many, many days.

Because of the hunter's resourcefulness and courage, the couple survived and prospered.

And that is the story of how one hunter outsmarted the great nanurluk.

CONTRIBUTORS

Jose Angutinngurniq was born at the head of an inlet after his parents returned from a walrus hunt in the area of Arviligjuaq, Nunavut. He grew up in the Natsilik region of Nunavut, around Taloyoak area, in a community called Ittuaqturvik. Jose first heard the story of *The Giant Bear* from his grandfather, Alakannuaq, who lived to be very old. When babies were born, the first person to hold the child became the sanaji, the one who forms the characteristics of the child. Alakannuaq formed Jose into who he is today. Jose chose to publish this story because it takes place around the coast of Taloyoak, where he grew up. When he was a younger man, Jose would tell legends and traditional stories to children, and that is what he is doing with this book, sharing a story that he loved.

Eva Widermann is a graduate of the graphic design program at the Academy of Fine Arts in Munich, Germany. She worked as a graphic designer for many years before she decided to pursue her long-term dream of becoming a freelance illustrator and concept artist. Her art is deeply influenced by an unusual combination of Franco-Belgian comics, manga, and anime. Eva has worked with Inhabit Media on various projects, including www.inuitmyths. com, to bring ancient Inuit mythology to life for a contemporary audience. She lives in Cork, Ireland.

APOLLO

God of the Sun, Healing, Music, and Poetry

BY TERI TEMPLE

ILLUSTRATED BY ROBERT SQUIER

Published by The Child's World®
1980 Lookout Drive • Mankato, MN 56003-1705
800-599-READ • www.childsworld.com

Acknowledgments
The Child's World®: Mary Berendes, Publishing Director
The Design Lab: Design and production
Red Line Editorial: Editorial direction

Design elements: Maksym Dragunov/Dreamstime;
Dreamstime

Photographs ©: Shutterstock Images, 5, 19, 20; S.Pytel/
Shutterstock Images, 12; Kamira/Shutterstock Images,
14; James Thew/Shutterstock Images, 24; Eric Isselée/
Shutterstock Images, 26; Georgios Alexandris/
Shutterstock Images, 29

ISBN 9781614732549
LCCN 2012932425

Printed in the United States of America
Mankato, MN
July 2012
PA02119

CONTENTS

INTRODUCTION, 4

CHARACTERS AND PLACES, 6

THE GOD OF MANY TALENTS, 8

PRINCIPAL GODS OF GREEK MYTHOLOGY—
A FAMILY TREE, 30

THE ROMAN GODS, 31

FURTHER INFORMATION, 32

INDEX, 32

INTRODUCTION

Long ago in ancient Greece and Rome, most people believed that gods and goddesses ruled their world. Storytellers shared the adventures of these gods to help explain all the mysteries in life. The gods were immortal, meaning they lived forever. Their stories were full of love and tragedy, fearsome monsters, brave heroes, and struggles for power. The storytellers wove aspects of Greek customs and beliefs into the tales. Some stories told of the creation of the world and the origins of the gods. Others helped explain natural events such as earthquakes and storms. People believed the tales, which over time became myths.

The ancient Greeks and Romans worshiped the gods by building temples and statues in their honor. They felt the gods would protect and guide them. People passed down the myths through the generations by word of mouth. Later, famous poets such as Homer and Hesiod wrote them down. Today, these myths give us a unique look at what life was like in ancient Greece more than 2,000 years ago.

ANCIENT GREEK SOCIETIES

IN ANCIENT GREECE, CITIES, TOWNS, AND THEIR SURROUNDING FARMLANDS WERE CALLED CITY-STATES. THESE CITY-STATES EACH HAD THEIR OWN GOVERNMENTS. THEY MADE THEIR OWN LAWS. THE INDIVIDUAL CITY-STATES WERE VERY INDEPENDENT. THEY NEVER JOINED TO BECOME ONE WHOLE NATION. THEY DID, HOWEVER, SHARE A COMMON LANGUAGE, RELIGION, AND CULTURE.

MOUNT OLYMPUS
The mountaintop home of the 12 Olympic gods

Aegean Sea

DELPHI, GREECE
A town in ancient Greece; home to Apollo's temple

ANCIENT GREECE

CRETE

OLYMPIAN GODS
Demeter, Hermes, Hephaestus, Aphrodite, Ares, Hera, Zeus, Poseidon, Athena, Apollo, Artemis, and Dionysus

TITANS (TIE-tinz)
The 12 children of Gaea and Cronus; godlike giants that are said to represent the forces of nature

APOLLO (a-POL-lo)
God of sun, music, healing, and prophecy; son of Zeus and Leto; twin to Artemis

ARTEMIS (AHR-tuh-mis)
Goddess of the hunt and the moon; daughter of Zeus and Leto; twin to Apollo

ASCLEPIUS
(as-KLEE-pee-uhs)
God of medicine; son of Apollo; killed by Zeus

6

CYCLOPES (SIGH-clopes)
One-eyed giants; children of Gaea and Uranus

DAPHNE (DAF-nee)
Nymph who was transformed into a laurel tree to escape Apollo

GAEA (JEE-uh)
Mother Earth and one of the first elements born to Chaos; mother of the Titans, Cyclopes, and Hecatoncheires

HERA (HEER-uh)
Queen of the gods; married to Zeus

HERMES (HUR-meez)
Messenger to the gods; god of travel and trade; son of Zeus

LETO (LEE-toh)
Titan goddess; wife of Zeus; mother of Apollo and Artemis

MARSYAS (MAHR-see-uhs)
Satyr who lost a music contest against Apollo

MIDAS (MY-duhs)
A king in ancient Greece known for his foolishness

MUSES (MYOOZ-ez)
The nine sister goddesses of the arts; attendants of Apollo

ORACLE OF DELPHI
(AWR-uh-kuhl of DEL-fahy)
A priestess who delivered the prophecies of Apollo

PHAETON (FAY-uh-thuhn)
Son of Helios; lost control driving the chariot of the sun and was struck down by Zeus

ZEUS (ZOOS)
Supreme ruler of the heavens and weather and of the gods who lived on Mount Olympus; youngest son of Cronus and Rhea; married to Hera; father of many gods and heroes

A pollo was a very powerful god in ancient Greece and Rome. He was the only god whose name was the same in both cultures. But, Apollo's story almost ended at his birth.

Mount Olympus was the mountaintop home of the Olympic gods. Hidden behind the clouds the gods watched over the heavens and Earth. It should have been a paradise. But things are not always as they seem.

Zeus was the king of the gods. He loved his beautiful wife Hera, but he wanted more wives and children. Hera was a jealous wife, though. She did not like sharing Zeus. So Zeus often snuck behind Hera's back to see his other wives and the beautiful maidens on Earth.

When Hera discovered that Zeus had married the Titan Leto, she was not very happy. Then she found out Leto was expecting twins. Hera was furious. She came up with a plan to get revenge. Hera made it so Leto would not find shelter anywhere on Earth. Then she sent her serpent Python after Leto. With no place to rest, Leto was chased from country to country. She thought she would never find a safe place to give birth to her twins.

Luckily for Leto, there was hope. Poseidon, the god of the seas, had just made a new island. He had yet to anchor it to the sea floor. As it was still floating on the water, Leto was not turned away. It was the island of Delos. There in the shade of its lone palm tree, Leto finally relaxed. But Hera was not finished with her just yet. Hera's daughter was Eileithyia. She was the goddess of childbirth. Hera refused to let her help Leto. Without Eileithyia's help, Leto could not give birth to her twins.

The other goddesses on Mount Olympus felt sorry for Leto. They wanted Hera to change her mind. They tempted Hera with a beautiful necklace of gold and amber. Hera could not resist their bribe. In exchange, Eileithyia was allowed to travel to the island. Leto finally gave birth to her babies.

First came Artemis, as lovely as the moon. She would become the goddess of the hunt and protector of all newborn creatures. Then came her twin brother Apollo, as glorious as the sun. He would become the god of the sun, music, healing, and prophecy. Zeus was joyful at the birth of his new son and daughter. He blessed the island. It became the richest of all the islands in Greece.

Apollo had many powers. He was the radiant god of the sun. But ancient Greeks felt Apollo was more than that. To them he was really the god of light and truth. The Greeks saw Apollo as a handsome young man. His garments were spun with gold and he traveled in his golden sun chariot. Apollo was a gifted archer, too. He often hunted with his sister Artemis.

As the god of music, Apollo spent his days entertaining the other gods on Mount Olympus. He would play his lyre for them. His lovely attendants were the Muses who played along with him. Apollo was also a skilled healer. He was the first to teach men the art of healing. His son Asclepius even became the Greek god of medicine.

Apollo was best known for being the god of prophecy. A prophecy is a prediction of what is to come. Apollo's gift made him a very popular god. Many people came to him seeking his advice. It was tiring for the god. Apollo decided he needed a helper.

HERMES AND THE LYRE

HERMES WAS THE GOD OF TRAVEL AND TRADE. AND HE WAS ALWAYS FULL OF MISCHIEF. WHEN HE WAS JUST A BABY, HE STOLE CATTLE THAT WERE BEING GUARDED BY

HIS BROTHER APOLLO. WHILE HIDING WITH THEM, HERMES USED A TORTOISE
SHELL TO MAKE THE FIRST LYRE. WHEN THE GODS CAUGHT HERMES HE BEGAN
TO PLAY IT. THE MUSIC WAS ENCHANTING TO APOLLO. HE AGREED TO FORGIVE
HERMES IN EXCHANGE FOR THE LYRE.

The ancient Greeks believed that it was wise to keep the gods happy. So they built temples in the gods' honor all over Greece. Each temple was special to just one god. Apollo's temple was built in the town of Delphi. There he put an oracle to speak on his behalf. The oracle was Pythia, a wise woman who could predict the future. Apollo gave her the gift of prophecy. But he limited her power. Pythia always had to tell the truth, but she could not answer with a yes or no. The listener had to guess Pythia's meaning. Sometimes her prophecies were hard to understand.

The oracle sat on her three-legged stool. She inhaled vapors that rose from a crack in the ground under her stool. Pythia would then tell her predictions while under a trance. Temple priests would help translate her prophecies. The ancient Greeks believed these were the words of Apollo. The temple at Delphi became one of the most important religious sites in Greece. It was also where the Pythian Games were held to honor Apollo.

PYTHIAN GAMES

THE PYTHIAN GAMES BEGAN IN THE SIXTH CENTURY BC. HELD EVERY FOUR YEARS, THEY WERE A MODEL FOR THE OLYMPIC GAMES. IT WAS AN IMPORTANT

SPORTING EVENT THAT ALSO INCLUDED MUSIC AND POETRY CONTESTS. ATHLETES FROM AROUND THE ANCIENT WORLD COULD SHOW OFF THEIR SKILLS. THE HIGHLIGHT OF THE GAMES WAS CHARIOT RACING. THE GREEKS EVEN BUILT A SPECIAL STADIUM FOR CHARIOT RACING CALLED A HIPPODROME.

Apollo was a master musician. The Olympic gods often asked him to play for them. The music he made was so lovely it caused them to forget all else. The Muses, nine sister goddesses, sang with Apollo. They added their beautiful voices as a chorus, filling the palace with music.

Each Muse was connected with a certain art or science. There was Mnemosyne, the goddess of memory. Next came the three sisters of poetry. Calliope's specialty was epic poems, Erato's was love poems, and Euterpe's was lyric poetry. The goddess of dance was Terpsichore. Polyhymnia favored sacred songs. There were also three goddesses of literature. Melpomene had tragedy, Thalia liked comedy, and Clio excelled in history. Finally there was Ourania, the goddess of astronomy.

Daughters of Zeus, the Muses helped humans be more creative. They inspired poetry, song, and dance. They were often asked for help as ancient Greek artists and writers began new works. Unlike many other gods, the Muses could see into the future. They remained young and beautiful forever.

Apollo and his sister Artemis were close friends as well as siblings. They both excelled at archery and enjoyed hunting together. The twin gods were also fiercely protective of their mother Leto. More than once, Apollo and Artemis punished those who dared insult Leto. Apollo went after the giant Tityus after he attacked Leto. He killed the giant with his deadly arrows. Tityus was then condemned to suffer in the underworld.

Python was also a target of Apollo's wrath. Apollo held a grudge against Python for chasing his mother. Then the serpent was set to guard the Oracle of Delphi. Apollo killed him when he took over the temple.

Niobe's tale was perhaps the most tragic. She foolishly mocked the goddess Leto for only having two children. Niobe then boasted that she had 14 children, seven sons and seven daughters. Apollo and Artemis were furious. Together they killed all 14 children. In grief, Niobe turned to stone and wept endless tears. It was not wise to anger the gods.

PYTHON

GAEA, OR MOTHER EARTH, CREATED THE SERPENT PYTHON. IT BECAME THE SWORN ENEMY OF APOLLO. HE BURIED THE SERPENT UNDER MOUNT PARNASSUS AFTER HE KILLED IT. THE BEAST INSPIRED THE NAME OF THE PRIESTESS OF APOLLO'S TEMPLE. SHE WAS KNOWN AS PYTHIA. APOLLO'S OWN FESTIVAL WAS NAMED THE PYTHIAN GAMES AFTER THE CREATURE.

Although he was handsome and talented, Apollo was not often lucky in love. The results of his attention were sometimes disastrous. One object of his affection was the river nymph Daphne. Eros, the god of love, had a hand in their bad luck. Eros was angry with Apollo for insulting his skills as an archer. So he shot a gold-tipped arrow at Apollo. It caused him to fall madly in love with Daphne. He then shot Daphne with a lead-tipped arrow. This caused her to hate any man who was in love with her.

Apollo was relentless in his chase of Daphne. Just as Apollo was about to catch Daphne, she sent a prayer up to Gaea. To help her escape, Gaea changed Daphne into a laurel tree. Apollo would never be able to have Daphne. Instead Apollo decided to make the laurel tree his sacred tree. He often wore a crown of laurel leaves on his head in Daphne's memory.

HYACINTHS

LEGENDS TELL THAT APOLLO AND ZEPHYRUS, GOD OF THE WEST WIND, WERE RIVALS. THEY BOTH WANTED TO BE FRIENDS WITH HYACINTHUS. ZEPHYRUS GREW

JEALOUS WHEN HE SAW APOLLO TEACHING HYACINTHUS TO THROW THE
DISCUS. A WIND GOD, ZEPHYRUS BLEW APOLLO'S DISC OFF COURSE. IT STRUCK
HYACINTHUS IN THE HEAD AND ACCIDENTALLY KILLED HIM. ANCIENT GREEKS
BELIEVED THAT APOLLO CAUSED THE FIRST HYACINTH FLOWER TO SPRING FROM
HYACINTHUS'S BLOOD.

Apollo was mostly a kind-hearted god. But he could be cruel if his musical skills were challenged. Marsyas was a satyr who dared to challenge Apollo. A satyr was a woodland creature that was half-human and half-horse or half-goat. Marsyas found an instrument in the woods. It was the flute the goddess Athena had invented. She did not like the way it made her look when she played it. So she threw it away. After composing many tunes, Marsyas felt he was good enough to compete against the god of music himself.

Marsyas played on his flute and Apollo on his lyre in a contest. After the first round, the contest was a draw. There was no winner or loser. Marsyas was indeed a fine musician. Apollo challenged him to a second round. The challenge was to play the instrument upside down. It was nearly impossible to play the flute upside down and Marsyas lost.

MIDAS AND HIS DONKEY EARS

MIDAS WAS AN ANCIENT GREEK KING KNOWN FOR HIS FOOLISHNESS. JUDGING A MUSICAL CONTEST BETWEEN APOLLO AND PAN. MIDAS AWARDED PAN THE PRIZE. OUT OF ANGER APOLLO CHANGED MIDAS'S EARS INTO DONKEY EARS. MIDAS

Apollo decided to punish Marsyas for his prideful boast. He tied Marsyas to a tree and had him punished terribly. Out of pity, the other gods changed Marsyas into a mountain stream.

TRIED TO HIDE THEM BUT FAILED WHEN HIS BARBER SAW HIS EARS. FEARING PUNISHMENT, MIDAS'S BARBER DUG A HOLE AND WHISPERED THE SECRET INTO THE GROUND. THE REEDS THAT GREW THERE WHISPERED MIDAS'S SECRET WHENEVER THE WIND BLEW.

The ancient Greeks believed the god of the sun made sure the sun rose and set each day. He did this by driving a golden chariot into the eastern sky at dawn. After driving the sun across the sky, the chariot went down into the west at the end of the day. That job had been assigned to the sun god Helios. Later Apollo became connected with Helios. They were sometimes considered to be the same god. Either way, the tragic youth Phaeton met his end in that chariot.

Phaeton was the son of the sun god. He begged to be allowed to drive the golden chariot just once. His father finally agreed. The path was steep and dangerous. Phaeton was not a very good driver. As a result, the horses ran wildly off course. When they came dangerously close to crashing into the earth, Zeus stepped in. He struck the chariot down with a thunderbolt. The river nymphs who found Phaeton's body mourned his death. He was placed among the stars as the constellation Auriga, or "the charioteer."

THE SUN

APOLLO IS OFTEN REFERRED TO AS THE GOD OF THE SUN. THE ACTUAL SUN IS A HUGE GLOWING STAR IN THE MILKY WAY GALAXY. THE SUN CAME INTO

EXISTENCE ABOUT 4.6 BILLION YEARS AGO. IT IS FOUND AT THE CENTER OF OUR SOLAR SYSTEM. THE OTHER PLANETS AND MOONS REVOLVE AROUND IT. THE SUN CREATES AN ENORMOUS AMOUNT OF ENERGY. IT PROVIDES THE EARTH WITH THE LIGHT AND HEAT NEEDED TO SUPPORT LIFE.

Apollo had another son. His name was Asclepius. Apollo rescued him from his mother's womb after she had died. Apollo gave the baby to the centaur Chiron to be raised. Under Chiron's care, Asclepius learned the art of healing. Asclepius became a gifted physician and surgeon. He was known as the god of medicine. As a gift, the goddess Athena gave Asclepius some of the Gorgon Medusa's blood. She was a monster with snakes on her head who could turn people to stone with her gaze. Her blood could be used for good or evil. Asclepius used his gift to raise a dead man back to life. Hades, the god of the underworld, complained to his brother Zeus. If Asclepius was allowed to raise the dead, Hades would lose subjects for the underworld. Therefore Zeus struck Asclepius down with his thunderbolt.

Apollo was furious with his father. In frustration, Apollo went after the Cyclopes. These giants had created the thunderbolt used to kill his son. By killing the Cyclopes, Apollo was trying to punish Zeus, who favored the giants. It did not bring Apollo's son back though.

KORONIS

WHEN THE PRINCESS KORONIS WAS PREGNANT WITH
APOLLO'S SON ASCLEPIUS, SHE FELL IN LOVE WITH
ANOTHER MAN. APOLLO DISCOVERED HER SECRET
FROM HIS RAVEN. IN ANGER HE SENT HIS SISTER

ARTEMIS AFTER KORONIS. ARTEMIS USED HER DEADLY ARROWS TO KILL KORONIS. BUT APOLLO WAS ABLE TO SAVE HIS SON ASCLEPIUS. ANCIENT GREEKS BELIEVED APOLLO PUNISHED THE RAVEN FOR TATTLING BY CHANGING ITS SNOW-WHITE FEATHERS TO BLACK.

Apollo was the image of the ideal man. He was smart, kind, youthful, and handsome. He was a gifted archer, musician, and healer. He could also tell the future. It is no wonder he became a symbol of perfection to the ancient Greeks. The Oracle of Delphi was considered to be the center of the world. Pilgrims came from many countries to seek answers. But more importantly they came to honor the god Apollo. To the ancient peoples, Apollo connected man with the gods. Apollo could guide them, help them make peace with the gods, and grant them pardon.

Apollo was a respected and loved god. He lives on through the stories and myths of the ancient Greeks and Romans who honored him.

DELPHI, GREECE

DELPHI WAS A TOWN IN ANCIENT GREECE. IT WAS LOCATED ON THE SOUTHERN SIDE OF MOUNT PARNASSUS. DELPHI WAS HOME TO THE ORACLE OF DELPHI. IT WAS SACRED TO THE GOD APOLLO. TO THE ANCIENT GREEKS IT WAS THE OLDEST AND MOST INFLUENTIAL RELIGIOUS SITE IN GREECE. INSCRIBED ON APOLLO'S TEMPLE THERE ARE THE FAMOUS EXPRESSIONS "KNOW THYSELF" AND "NOTHING IN EXCESS." ONLY REMAINS OF THE TEMPLE CAN BE SEEN TODAY.

PRINCIPAL GODS OF GREEK MYTHOLOGY –
A FAMILY TREE

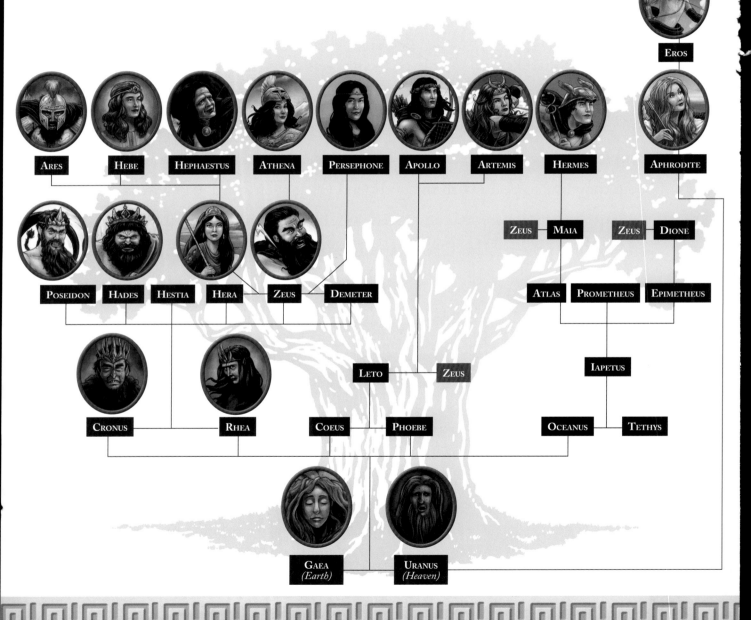

EROS

ARES | HEBE | HEPHAESTUS | ATHENA | PERSEPHONE | APOLLO | ARTEMIS | HERMES | APHRODITE

ZEUS — MAIA | ZEUS — DIONE

POSEIDON | HADES | HESTIA | HERA | ZEUS | DEMETER | ATLAS | PROMETHEUS | EPIMETHEUS

IAPETUS

LETO — ZEUS

CRONUS | RHEA | COEUS | PHOEBE | OCEANUS — TETHYS

GAEA
(Earth) | URANUS
(Heaven)

THE ROMAN GODS

As the Roman Empire expanded by conquering new lands the Romans often took on aspects of the customs and beliefs of the people they conquered. From the ancient Greeks they took their arts and sciences. They also adopted many of their gods and the myths that went with them into their religious beliefs. While the names were changed, the stories and legends found a new home.

ZEUS: *Jupiter*
King of the Gods, God of Sky and Storms
Symbols: *Eagle and Thunderbolt*

HERA: *Juno*
Queen of the Gods, Goddess of Marriage
Symbols: *Peacock, Cow, and Crow*

POSEIDON: *Neptune*
God of the Sea and Earthquakes
Symbols: *Trident, Horse, and Dolphin*

HADES: *Pluto*
God of the Underworld
Symbols: *Helmet, Metals, and Jewels*

ATHENA: *Minerva*
Goddess of Wisdom, War, and Crafts
Symbols: *Owl, Shield, and Olive Branch*

ARES: *Mars*
God of War
Symbols: *Vulture and Dog*

ARTEMIS: *Diana*
Goddess of Hunting and Protector of Animals
Symbols: *Stag and Moon*

APOLLO: *Apollo*
God of the Sun, Healing, Music, and Poetry
Symbols: *Laurel, Lyre, Bow, and Raven*

HEPHAESTUS: *Vulcan*
God of Fire, Metalwork, and Building
Symbols: *Fire, Hammer, and Donkey*

APHRODITE: *Venus*
Goddess of Love and Beauty
Symbols: *Dove, Sparrow, Swan, and Myrtle*

EROS: *Cupid*
God of Love
Symbols: *Quiver and Arrows*

HERMES: *Mercury*
God of Travels and Trade
Symbols: *Staff, Winged Sandals, and Helmet*

FURTHER INFORMATION

BOOKS

Green, Jen. *Ancient Greek Myths*. New York: Gareth Stevens, 2010.

Napoli, Donna Jo. *Treasury of Greek Mythology: Classic Stories of Gods, Goddesses, Heroes & Monsters*. Washington, DC: National Geographic Society, 2011.

Orr, Tamra. *Apollo*. Hockessin, DE: Mitchell Lane Publishers, 2009.

WEB SITES

Visit our Web site for links about Apollo:
childsworld.com/links

Note to Parents, Teachers, and Librarians: We routinely verify our Web links to make sure they are safe and active sites. So encourage your readers to check them out!

INDEX

ancient Greek society, 5, 12, 14, 16, 24, 27, 29
Apollo,
    attendants, 12, 16
    birth, 8, 10
    children, 12, 24, 26, 27
    cruelty, 19, 22–23
    love, 20, 26
    music, 10, 12, 13, 16, 22, 29
    parents, 8, 10, 16, 19, 24, 26
    siblings, 10, 12, 13, 19, 27
    talents, 12–13, 20
    temple of, 14, 19, 29
Artemis, 10, 12, 19, 27
Asclepius, 12, 26, 27
Athena, 22, 26
Auriga constellation, 24

Chiron, 26
Cyclopes, 26
Daphne, 20
Delos, 10
Delphi, 14, 19, 29
Eileithyia, 10
Eros, 20
Gaea, 19, 20
Hades, 26
Helios, 24
Hera, 8, 10
Hermes, 12–13
hyacinths, 20–21
Hyacinthus, 20–21
Koronis, 26–27
Leto, 8, 10, 19
Marsyas, 22–23

Medusa, 26
Midas, 22–23
Mount Olympus, 8, 10, 12
Mount Parnassus, 19, 29
Muses, 12, 16
Niobe, 19
Phaeton, 24
Poseidon, 10
Pythia, 14, 19, 29
Pythian Games, 14, 19
Python, 8, 19
storytellers, 5
sun, 10, 12, 24–25
Tityus, 19
Zephyrus, 20–21
Zeus, 8, 10, 16, 24, 26